Thelma's Boy

Thelma's Boy

George L. Allen

To order additional copies of this book, contact:
Xlibris Corporation
1-888-795-4274
www.Xlibris.com
Orders@Xlibris.com
69338

Chapter One

My name is Jake Hamilton. But the people around our Amarillo, Texas, neighborhood call me Thelma's Boy. The only reason I can think of for this nickname is me and my mama have always been close. She is my best friend, and I've never doubted her love, even though she can be mighty strict with me sometimes.

To give you a better idea about my mama, let me tell you something that happened a while ago that clearly shows what kind of woman my mama is.

About nine o'clock one Spring morning in 1940, I was so busy having fun I didn't realize one of the old neighborhood ladies had spotted me doing something she thought was awfully bad. She caught me holding a kicking, scratching, squalling cat by the scruff of its neck. While dodging the cat's claws and teeth, I was trying to tie some tin cans I'd rigged up to the poor critter's tail. As soon as that old biddy saw and heard what I was doing, she hightailed it over to my house and told my mama.

A few minutes later, when I heard Mama call my name "Jaaaaa-eeeek!" in that special tone she used when she was angry, I could tell I was in big trouble. I got myself ready for a whale of a smacking. After what I'd done to that poor cat, I was sure Mama would make me go find her a big switch, and when she got through with me, my backside was going to be sore for a week.

However, on this particular day, I got a pleasant surprise. Mama didn't give me the spanking I expected. I guess she must've been too tired and thought that switching a little ruffian like me would take too much energy.

Instead of her using a switch on me, my punishment was going to be something Mama knew I dreaded. It was something she knew would hurt me more than just a little old spanking. She was going to make me stop playing and come inside. Hanging my head down, and putting on my most penitent look, I trudged toward the front of the house a little unwillingly, knowing I was going to miss being outside. In my little boy's heart, I felt like a prisoner being led away to prison. My life was about to come apart, all because that old meddling snoop down the street hadn't minded her own business and kept her mouth shut.

As we walked, Mama grabbed me by the seat of my pants, almost lifting me off the ground. As she pushed and pulled me toward the house, she made my legs kick first one way and then the other. While all this ruckus was happening, I was thinking about the treachery of that old meddlesome busybody who had gotten me into all this trouble. Although I knew it wasn't a nice thing to think or do, I found myself wishing I could find a way to get even with the nosy old biddy by putting some tin cans on her.

When we got to the front of the house, Mama shoved me headfirst through the front door. "And you stay in there until you feel sorry for what you did!" she shouted. Since I didn't feel sorry, I figured I was going to be in the house for a long time, perhaps for the rest of my life. I felt terribly unhappy.

Once I got inside, I looked around our small, sparsely furnished living room for something to do. On the table next to the couch, I saw something that hadn't been there before: a big red book. Its pages were dog-eared, and it was called The Count of Monte Cristo. Mama had gotten it from Miss Millie, one of the white ladies she worked for.

After I began reading the book, I knew after the first pages that I was hooked. I could tell I was going to like this book because the further I got into it, the more it gave me the chance to be the hero when I wanted, or the nasty villain if I found that more convenient. Once I started reading, I couldn't put the old book down. I just kept turning the pages.

While the sun shone through the windows, I lay on the floor, reading. When it got dark, I ambled over to the chair next to the big yellow lamp in our front room. I settled back down on the floor and continued reading, so captivated by the book that I had no awareness of the passing of time.

Three or four hours must have gone by when Mama called me. I was so into that book I didn't even hear her. When she noticed I didn't answer—that I was, in fact, paying no attention to her—she walked up to where I was lying on the floor. Pulling one of my ears, she said, "Time to eat, boy. Put that book down."

"Yes'm," I answered.

As I sat down to eat, I felt strange, almost as if I'd experienced a little miracle. I was amazed at the change that had come over me. I'd always been blessed with a robust appetite and as far back as I could remember, I'd never been late for supper or any other meal. But today, I felt different. Reading had made me forget eating. But what was even stranger than that, reading had made me forget that I was being punished. I popped a biscuit into my mouth and used the back of my right hand to wipe the milk-stain from my top lip. I felt so good. As some new thoughts whizzed through my head, I couldn't help saying one of them aloud: "I guess I found myself a new way to have some real good fun!"

Next morning when I got up, I threw my clothes on and rushed into the front room. That old, faded, dog-eared book was still there, so I picked it up and started reading again. Lying on the floor, I must have read ten or twenty pages when Mama came into the room. "You still reading, Son?"

When I nodded and showed her the book, I could tell she was happy. The grin she had on her face lit up the whole room.

"Mama," I said, as I rested on my elbow. "While I was reading, I noticed something about this here old book—some of the pages are sticking together. How'd that happen? Did somebody put some glue on them?"

Mama chuckled and patted me on the head. She was a short, chubby little lady, with smooth brown skin. Whether she was happy or sad, she made her feelings jump from her to the person she was talking to. That morning, she wore a green dress and a white apron, and it made her look cheerful and homey.

"I did that," she said. "And that ain't no glue. That's honey."

Because I just assumed the book was mine and nobody else's, I could feel my face getting really hot when she told me what had happened to the book. So I said, "Why'd you go and do that, Mama? Why'd you get the pages all messy and sticky with honey?"

"Well, son." She rubbed both her hands on her apron. "I was so proud when I saw how you took to that book last night. It made me feel real good. So I got to thinking about how I could encourage you to keep on reading."

Mama shuffled over to the red chair in the corner of the room and sat down. Folding her hands on her lap, she continued.

"I thought to myself, why not put some honey on the pages of this old book? And when the boy wakes up in the morning and asks me why I did it, I'll tell him." Mama stood, lifting herself to her fullest height. With her right hand, she scratched the side and back of her head.

"Son, I'll say." She paused a moment. "I put honey on these here pages, so you'll remember something very important."

"What do you want me to remember, Mama?"

She put her hands in the pockets of her apron. Her voice seemed to flaunt the pride she felt. "Child, long after I'm dead and gone, I want you to remember that knowledge is sweet."

"Knowledge is sweet?" I repeated, shaking my head.

As soon as the words left my mouth, and I saw the quizzical look on Mama's face, I realized I'd done something I shouldn't ought to do. Since Mama bragged about me to everybody, and told them I was a smart little fellow, I couldn't let her know I didn't understand what she meant when she did all that talking about knowledge. So to keep my secret that I was puzzled and bewildered by her words, I grabbed and caressed Mama's hands. This affectionate routine usually made Mama smile. I knew it had worked again when I saw the delighted twinkle darting from her eyes. So, in my most enthusiastic voice I said, "Thank you, Mama." And from a kneeling position, while she stood above me, I hugged her.

Then I rolled over on my belly, opened my book, and started reading.

I hadn't finished more than a page or two when Mama came back.

"Boy," she said, "you been fooling with that book long enough today.

Don't you see that sun ashining out there?"

"Yes'm, I do."

"Then you get on up, put that book down and go on outside for a while."

Remembering the fun I had yesterday before I got caught teasing that old ugly cat, I did what Mama told me. Reluctantly, I put the book on the floor next to the couch. The thought of Edmond Dante made me smile. In my mind's eye, I could see the hero of my book sailing into the port of Marseilles, hoping to find a new life full of promise and joy. As I thought about the happiness he expected, I made my way to the front door and went outside.

Chapter Two

When I got outside, I saw Daddy. He was a tall, black man, with velvety skin and huge rippling muscles in his arms. One of his legs hung over the side of a stool. As he strummed his guitar and sang one of his made-up songs, he tapped his foot and shook his head from side to side. Because he closed his eyes while he played and sang, Daddy seemed lost in the ecstasy of his music. As I watched him—too fascinated to speak—I had the feeling he didn't even know I had come outside. When I said, "Hello, Daddy," he opened his eyes.

He seemed disappointed for a moment. Then, motioning to me he said, "Come here, boy."

Daddy took a piece of paper out of his shirt pocket. "Son, your mama gave me this here list of things she wants from the store. I'm too tired and I don't feel like going." He leaned his guitar on the stool and reached into his pocket and took out his wallet. He removed a folded bill and spoke in a gruff voice:

"You take this here dollar and this here list and you go get your mama some eggs and some frying sausages." Then sitting down on his stool, he paused before asking, "Think you can do that?"

"Yes, Sir." I stuffed the money and the list in my pocket. "Can I get me some bubble gum?"

"Yeah, I suppose you can—if you can get it for a penny."

Walking toward the street, I felt real important and all grown up. I had been eight years old for only a short time, and I remember thinking that I must be getting to be a big boy. Otherwise, why else would Daddy trust me to go to the store all by myself with this great big dollar bill? I skipped along the road, smiling because I was so happy inside.

I must have walked three or four blocks from my house when I met Charlie Brown, T. J. Cook and Billy Crawford—three of my neighborhood playmates. Playing marbles next to an old, boarded-up house, they had drawn a large circle on the ground with a big wide stick. Although I usually lost at marbles, I still wanted to play. I felt my luck was going to be good on this particular day. So I shoved my hand into my left pocket—the one that didn't have the money and the note—and found almost a dozen marbles, two or three of them prized and colorful agates.

When I asked my buddies if I could join them, one of them said, "Yeah, I guess you can." So I knelt down and, with my knuckles touching the ground, I took my turn shooting at the marbles in the middle of the circle.

It didn't take my playmates long to clean me out. After we finished the game and they had won every marble I had, I got ready to continue my trip to the store. When I stood, I reached down into my right pocket. The money and the note Daddy had given me had, like a ghost, disappeared. When I accused my playmates of stealing the money, T. J. Cook denied it, and in a mocking voice said, "We didn't even know you had any money, Stupid."

On the long trip back home, I shoved both hands into empty pockets. Tears welled up in my eyes, and my face drooped. I shuffled along the road, not knowing what I was going to do or say. If I couldn't find that money, I felt sure Daddy would want to kill me.

Because I wanted to postpone going back home as long as I could, I moseyed around for a while, wandering over towards the Amarillo Ice House, not too far from where I lived. Then I went down to the place we boys called "the jungle." At night, in one of the ponds down there, some of my buddies and I spent a lot of time killing frogs. How helpless those frogs had seemed. After we shined flashlights in their eyes, they became paralyzed, inviting us to bop them upside the head with a stick and then stab them with some short spears we'd made from somebody's abandoned metal coat-hangers. After a while, when I didn't find anybody in the jungle,

I mustered enough courage to continue my long trek back home. I couldn't help but think how like those frogs I was at that moment. As I made my way home, like them, I felt helpless and paralyzed.

When I got back to the house, the sun had gone down, and the lights in the house had been turned on. Daddy had picked up his stool and guitar and gone inside. Since I was scared, I must have stood outside for more than an hour. Then, because I was getting cold and hungry, I burst inside the house and blurted out to Mama and Daddy what had happened.

"You did what?" Daddy howled. His voice sounded high, almost like a yelp.

I sobbed as I tried to explain. "On the way to the store, I played marbles. When we finished the game, I couldn't find the note and the money you gave me. They just disappeared. I don't know what happened to them."

Daddy stood. "You come on out to the backyard, young man."

He strode towards the back of the house, pulling the big black belt he wore through the loops of his trousers. "I'm going to learn you a lesson."

Outside, Daddy grabbed my left hand and began to whack me with that ugly black belt. Each lick felt like I had been struck by lightning.

"Daddy, I won't do it no more!" I shrieked. "I won't do it no more!"

My daddy must have hit me twelve or fifteen licks before he was satisfied. By then his blue shirt was soaked with sweat across his back and under his arms. When he thought he had laid enough licks on me, he shoved me toward the house. "Now you get on back inside."

Tears streamed down my face, as I stumbled back into the house, bawling as loud as I could. My back and my butt felt like they had been set on fire.

Later that night, after all the excitement, I lay on my cot next to the stove, on top of the covers, sore all over. Even though I hurt whenever I moved, I kept my ears open to hear Mama and Daddy talking in the front room.

"Why'd you whip the boy so hard?" Mama asked. She kept her voice low and soft, but I could tell she was mad at Daddy. But she didn't want to get him riled up. She knew that when he became too upset about anything, he could become unreasonable, and sometimes violent, even with her.

"That boy's got no head on his shoulders," Daddy said. "Maybe my belt will learn him a thing or two, make him think before he acts the next time."

"But why'd you whip him so hard?"

"Somehow that boy's got to realize just how hard I have to work for a dollar. I make ten cents an hour, working ten hours a day. That's a whole day's pay that boy's done gone and thrown away." Then, in his most soothing voice, he said, "Thelma, honey,"—Daddy used Mama's name and called her honey when he wanted her understanding and forgiveness. "I guess I whipped the boy hard 'cause I was mad—and maybe that's not right. But how else will he learn what a dollar means unless I teach him?" When he said these last words, to me they sounded like the alien words of a stranger who had made no attempt to get to know me.

"Go talk to the boy in the morning," Mama said. Her voice had a soothing, yet cutting quality to it, and I knew she was using her voice—and her words—to make Daddy feel guilty about the whipping.

"Oh, all right. I guess no harm can come from doing that."

The next day before Daddy went to work, he came to where I slept. Sitting next to me on my cot, he put his hands on my shoulders. "Son, I want you to know that yesterday when I whipped you, I didn't whip you for losing the money."

"You didn't, Daddy?" I remembered he had grimaced and twisted his lips as he laid each heavy lick on my back.

"No, no, son. It wasn't the money at all." Drawing out and expanding each word until it took him almost forever to say it, he told me in a voice barely above a whisper: "I whipped you for stopping."

There was a moment of silence between us. He stared at me. Despite his attempts to be nice, Daddy's gaze hardened and kept me from looking him in the face. I held my head down, adjusted my pajama top and patted my pillow.

"From now on," he continued, "whenever I send you somewhere, I want you to go and come on back. Don't you stop to play marbles. Don't you stop to play nothing."

Then Daddy stood. He moved his fingers through the loops of his belt, adjusting his pants so that he could leave for work. By the way his deep voice rose, I knew he must have been thinking about the dollar bill I had lost.

"Do you understand what I mean?" he asked.

"Yes, Sir." I forced my eyes to meet his. He gritted his teeth and the veins in his temples stood out. Deep furrows lay in rows on his forehead, and he didn't have even a trace of a smile.

"I understand what you mean, Sir."

As Daddy made his way through the living room and out the front door, I felt like I didn't have any friends left in the world. That's when I reached down beside my cot to pick up my faded old buddy, *The Count of Monte Cristo*. Within minutes, I was caught up in that exciting story again. I escaped into the mysterious pages and forgot about losing the money and the note. I forgot about losing my agates to my friends. I even forgot about the pain I felt from Daddy's hard licks. I read until my eyelids grew heavy. Then, before I laid it down to take the long nap Mama had told me to take, I squeezed and hugged that old, red, dog-eared book—just as I would squeeze and hug a trusted friend.

Chapter Three

When I went to Frederick Douglass School the next morning, my back was still a little sore, but I didn't complain. In fact, when I met and talked with my buddies at school, I laughed and smiled a lot so nobody would know how much pain and shame I felt.

I had some trouble sitting straight at my desk. I kept the palms of my hands on the sides of my face so I could give all my attention to Mrs. Graves, our third grade teacher. Mrs. Graves had a good lesson going on this day. Her eyes jumped out at you stern and grey, and even though her hair was white and fluffy and her ebony skin wrinkled with age, her musical voice kept us students looking up at her, wide-eyed and spellbound.

She was reading a chapter from Frederick Douglass's book, where he talks about his life. When she got to that part where Douglass tricked his white playmates into helping him learn to read, I took my hands from the sides of my face and listened hard to every word Mrs. Graves read. When she finished, Mrs. Graves lifted her eyeglasses to her forehead. Then she placed her book on the edge of her desk, stepped to the middle of the classroom and smiled.

"So you see, boys and girls, when you get hungry for knowledge, like Frederick Douglass, you will do almost anything to get it. You boys and girls don't know it now, but knowledge is going to be very important in your lives." Then, pursing her lips and putting her hands in the pockets of her polka-dot dress, she said, "How many of you boys and girls are willing to do something for me?"

All our hands shot up.

"Well, I want you to show me that you're hungry for knowledge. I want you to study real hard. Then you can go out into the world and find a place for yourselves. Are you willing to do that for me?" As she hurled this challenge, Mrs. Graves smiled again. Eager to please her and not wanting anything to dampen our enthusiasm, we chimed in, "Yes ma'am!"

I really thought Mrs. Graves had taught us a good lesson, and during the fifteen minute recess, ideas about Frederick Douglass raced around in my head. In my mind, I could see old Fred as a boy, leaving his dank cabin in the slave quarters, doing his best to try to figure out what he was going to learn that day, and how he was going to charm his white playmates into teaching it to him. Completely captivated, I must have been lost in my thoughts when something happened to bring me quickly back to reality. I heard the raucous, intimidating voice of Jim Willie Ross and saw him walking fast over to one of the water fountains where I was standing. Panic stricken, I tried to get away, but he caught up with me and shoved me against the wall. "Hey, you knucklehead," he said. "How much money you got?"

"I only got a nickel," I said.

"Give it to me, you lunkhead!"

"No! I ain't going to do it. If I give you my nickel, I won't be able to buy nothing for lunch."

"If you don't give me that nickel, Mouseface, when school's out, I'm going to kick your butt."

The bell rang, ending the recess. Before he swaggered away, Jim Willie shoved me again, making my shoulders and back hit the wall with a resounding thud.

"I'm going to get you after school," Jim Willie said as he slipped away down the hall. "I'm going to get you, Mouseface! Just you wait!"

When I went back to class, I was so agitated I couldn't focus on what the teacher was saying. All I heard was the drone of her voice. When I kept squirming around in my seat, Mrs. Graves came over and asked, "What's wrong with you, boy? Why can't you sit still?"

Not wanting to let her know about my recess encounter with Jim Willie, I told her, "I don't know, ma'am. I don't know what's wrong."

"Well, you better be still and keep quiet, or I'll have to send you out of the room. You're disturbing the rest of the class."

When school was over that day, I was the first to leave, which was a little out of character for me. Usually, I lingered a bit after school, playing and talking with some of my buddies. But on this day, I figured if I couldn't beat Jim Willie in a fight, then maybe I could outrun him. I must have walked a pretty good piece down the road when Jim Willie suddenly jumped from behind one of the houses. The only way he could have beaten me to that spot was if he'd played hooky during the last period. Also, apparently, he knew the way I walked home.

"I told you I was going to get you," he said, as he lashed out at me with balled-up fists.

When one of his blows landed on my nose, and another above my right eye, I screamed, "Jim Willie, I ain't going to give you my money. I ain't going to do it!"

"Give me that nickel, Ratface, or I'll bop you again!"

I broke away from him and ran as fast as I could. I could hear Jim Willie panting behind me, in hot pursuit. As we both dashed down the road, it became obvious that I had guessed right: I was faster than Jim Willie, and he really had no chance of catching me. When I thought I had left him behind, Jim Willie picked up a rock and hurled it at me. When the rock hit the back of my head, I screamed. But I kept on running. The next thing I knew, I was crying and scrambling through the front door of my house. Mama, who had been standing in the front room, grabbed me. "What in the world happened to you, son?"

I started bawling, cradling my head on her bosom. Mama wrapped her big arms around me. Then, patting me on my shoulder, she led me to the kitchen where she heated some water. She used a hot, wet cloth to soothe the pain and wipe away the blood.

Later that evening, Daddy came home from work. After he took one look at the gash over my eye and the hickey on the back of my head, he became furious.

"What happened to you?"

"Jim Willie Ross caught me after school and beat me up."

"Didn't you fight him back?"

"Daddy, he didn't give me a chance. I had to run from him."

"Well, I can see now you got to learn to fight."

Daddy told me to go outside to the backyard. "We still have a few hours left before the sun goes down," he said. "We got just enough time for me to learn you how to protect yourself."

Mama, who was watching both of us with a worried look on her face, told my daddy, "Now, Zeke, don't you go and hurt that boy. He's already been hurt enough today. You be careful now."

"Aw, woman," Daddy said. "You let me take care of this. It's my job as a man to make sure nobody runs over my son. It's time he learned how to handle himself."

I did as Daddy told me and went out to the backyard. Pretty soon, after he had drunk his evening cup of coffee, Daddy came out.

"Okay, young fellow, raise up your arms and hands."

When I did as Daddy told me, he said, "No, no! Not like that. Like this."

Then, after demonstrating where he wanted me to hold my hands, he showed me how to throw some punches with my balled-up fists and how to keep my balance as I was swinging.

"Okay, it's about time for you and me to box a little. You play like you're Joe Louis and put your hands up. Come at me as hard and as fast as you can."

"Daddy, I don't want to learn to fight," I protested.

"Okay, if you won't come after me, then I'm going to have to come after you."

When I didn't budge, Daddy popped me on the side of the face with the palm of his right hand, bringing tears to my eyes.

"I don't want to fight, Daddy," I complained. "I'm scared—and Jim Willie's mean. He likes going around hurting people. I don't. I ain't like that at all."

"Shut up," Daddy told me. The tears he saw on the sides of my cheeks must have made him agitated again because I could see him gritting his teeth and grimacing as he usually did when he was upset. "You ain't nothing but a goddamn crybaby. You got to be a man out here in this world. You can't go 'round crying all the time. You too big and too old for that."

He grabbed me roughly around my shoulders. "Now you listen to me. The next time you want to cry, I want you to hush it up. Turn it off. Keep your tears to yourself. Be a man."

After Daddy turned me loose, he hauled off and bopped me again with his open hand. In a fit of anger, I lunged at him, swinging at his head with all my might. I was so crazy with rage that I was hoping my blows would be strong enough to tear my daddy's head off.

"Hey, now, that's better," Daddy said. "I knew you had some fight in you." He put his hands on my shoulders again.

"Boy, if you can throw some licks like that, the next time you meet up with Jim Willie, you ought to be able to knock him into the middle of next week."

I swung one more hard punch, but Daddy stopped the blow in midair in the palm of his left hand. Then he grabbed me and gave me a hug.

"Okay, little champ, that's enough for one lesson." He winked at me and draped his arms around my shoulders. He was no longer gritting his teeth. In fact, as we walked back into the house I noticed, through tear-filled eyes, that my daddy had a smile on his face.

Chapter Four

The next day after my dad gave me my first boxing lesson, I felt a little better about myself. But I was still afraid to meet up with Jim Willie. I knew just what he would do the next time he saw me. After cornering me, he would grab my shoulders, shake me, slap me, kick me, and then punch me in the face. He had done this at least three times in the past, and I had a feeling that nothing had happened since we last met that would change his approach to me. He knew I was afraid of him, and he did everything he could to take advantage of this fear.

Jim Willie and I were the same age—eight years old—but he was huskier, stronger, and much more aggressive. There was something downright mean about Jim Willie. Fighting brought a glow to his eyes and allowed him to exert his will over me and all the other boys in the neighborhood.

When Daddy was teaching me to box, he kept reminding me how important it was for a man to stand up and fight. "I tell you, boy," he said, "if you don't throw some punches at Jim Willie, he'll be kicking your butt for breakfast, lunch and dinner."

As Daddy was telling me this, I became upset. I didn't like the way he completely discounted and made fun of how I felt about Jim Willie and about fighting. Anyway, to make sure I understood him, Daddy gave me an ultimatum, pointing and shaking his finger so that it almost touched my nose. His thunderous voice made his meaning clear. "If you let that Jim Willie beat you up again, when I get home, you're going to have another whipping coming—this time from me." Daddy shook his head and made fists with both his hands.

"I'm telling you, boy, if old Jim Willie bothers you again, you'd better fight him like your life depended on it. Otherwise, when I come home and find out you didn't slug it out with him, I'm going to set your tail on fire."

When I left my house on my way to school, I could still hear Daddy's threatening words. But this didn't keep me from being scared. My fear made me hope that Jim Willie would be sick or something that day so I wouldn't have to meet him. But my luck didn't hold. Before I had walked a block or two from my house, I saw old Jim Willie coming towards me, swaggering down the road like he owned it.

"Hey, you!" he shouted. "What you got there?" He pointed at the small, brown paper bag I held in my right hand. I knew it was too late to hide the bag, so I told him it contained some pork-sausage sandwiches Mama had made for my lunch.

"Give me that bag, sucker," Jim Willie sneered.

"No, no, Jim Willie!" I backed away from him. "I can't do that!"

"Give me that bag, you hear? Or I'll put my fists upside your head!"

"No, Jim Willie!" I stumbled away from him. "I don't care what you do. I ain't going to give you my lunch."

"I said gimme that bag!" Jimmy shouted and lunged at me, with his fists flailing, and grunting as he threw each punch.

When I remembered Daddy's ultimatum, I dropped the bag and grabbed Jim Willie around his shoulders. Both of us huffed and puffed and punched and tugged at each other for several minutes, and I surprised myself by holding my own. That morning I discovered that contrary to what I believed, Jim Willie was not all that invincible when I fought back.

Suddenly, during our struggle, we both fell. Jim Willie's leg was stretched straight as a tree-limb under me, and I heard it pop when we tumbled to the ground. Jim Willie screamed as he grabbed his leg. Then he started bawling as we both watched blood saturate the leg of the blue corduroy pants he was wearing. When I saw Jim Willie's leg and frightened eyes and heard him screaming and crying, I scooped up my bag of sausage sandwiches and hustled home as fast as I could. I was hollering at the top of my lungs, "Jim Willie's leg's broken! Jim Willie's leg's broken!

When the folks on the block heard my shouting, they rushed from their houses and ran to where Jim Willie sat, frightened and crying. Pretty soon, somebody pulled up in a car, swooped Jim Willie up and rushed him to the hospital.

Later that evening, my parents went to see Jim Willie in the hospital.

His leg was in a big white cast and, according to Mama and Daddy, Jim Willie's demeanor was uncharacteristically contrite. Daddy later told me that, from the way Jim Willie looked, nobody would ever guess that this little fellow had been terrorizing the neighborhood. Because he tried, most of the time, to be a reasonable man, Daddy agreed to pay Jim Willie's doctor bill. Mama told me he had said, "It's going to be worth the money to keep that ornery, little rascal from fighting all the time."

Mama, who didn't like violence, scolded me a little because she didn't approve of me being in a fight that had resulted in the breaking of a little boy's leg. On the other hand, Daddy seemed prouder of me than he had ever been. When he got home from the hospital that night, he came and sat down next to me on my cot. He fidgeted a little and then he said, "Today you did a good job, son. You stood up and fought. Even though old Jim Willie's leg got broke, you took a big step in becoming a man."

Daddy smiled and stood up to get ready to go back to the front room. He reached out suddenly and thumped me on my chin with his forefinger. This gesture, which to him must have been suggestive of a manly caress, had me grinning and squirming from an ecstasy I didn't quite understand. When I fell asleep that night, I felt happier than I had in a long time.

The next day, as I walked out of my house, the fear that had held me captive for so long was noticeably gone. I wasn't the scared little boy I had once been. I could sense a change in demeanor and outlook by the proud way I held my shoulders and by the new, cocky strut I had developed in my walk. I guess I was brimming all over with confidence because I knew that even when Jim Willie got back from the hospital with a cast on his leg, I wouldn't have to worry about him ever beating me up again. As I walked along the road that day, with bright eyes and a glowing smile, I felt like I was going to have some peace for a while.

Chapter Five

After the boxing lesson, when my daddy hugged me, he made me feel real good. His hug and the way he slung his arms around my shoulders—like I was his real buddy—made me forget the pain from his open-handed smacks upside my head. And after that first boxing session was over, when I noticed the smile escaping from his lips and the look of satisfaction on his face, I began to feel it might just be possible for me to do something that would make Daddy like me.

After I overcame my paralyzing fear of Jim Willie Ross, I became confused. Although the facts were staring me in the face, it was still hard for me to see that Daddy was right. Even though I never lost my deep-seated hatred for violence, I had to admit that my life was much better after I learned something about fighting. I learned that Jim Willie and all the other bullies like him weren't so tough after all. I proved that I could hold my own in a fight with Jim Willie Ross; in such a fight, I could deal out as much punishment as I had to take.

So even though I didn't want to at first, I had to conclude that Daddy wasn't such a bad guy after all. I couldn't deny that it was Daddy who taught me how to protect myself. I could see that when he was teaching me, although he did it in a rough way, he was proving that he really liked me. Maybe he even loved me. I felt giddy when he gave me one of his rationed smiles, and I began to think that it might just be possible for Daddy and me to become real friends. Oh, my goodness, I thought. If that could happen, I would be so happy. Why, if I could have me a daddy to love just like all the other kids on the block, I would have a grin on my face all the time.

But I should have known my good luck and good feelings couldn't last.

I began to see another mean side of my daddy again when, one Saturday, about 9:30 in the morning, he stalked in from work and saw me lying on the living room floor reading.

I thought he was going to encourage me and give me a sermon like Mama always did—about how important knowledge was. However, instead of praising me, Daddy spoke to me in a voice that sounded like he was angry or upset about something:

"What you doing, boy?"

"I'm reading, Sir. I'm almost finished reading this here book."

"What in hell do you expect to get out of all that reading?"

"Well, Mama told me books would get me some knowledge. She told me that knowledge was sweet and that it would give me some freedom one day."

"I don't care what your mama told you, boy," Daddy said. "Books ain't worth a damn. They ain't worth the paper they're printed on. They ain't going to help you, or anybody else, make a dime. They're just a waste of time. Instead of laying here on the floor reading some damn book, you should be outside trying to find a job. I know you only eight years old, but you need to be learning now how to make a dollar."

Daddy was so angry, he was shaking.

"That's what I was doing when I was your age—working. One day you're going to be a family man, and that's why you need to be doing something about it right now." Daddy scratched his head and put his hand on his chin. "Right now, you need to be getting some experience by shining shoes or working in the bowling alley, or doing something—so you can learn what it takes to put some food in your children's belly."

"But Daddy, I ain't a man yet. I'm just a little boy and I like to read." I got up on one knee when I told him this. "It's one way I can have some fun. I can learn about so many good things." I paused, looking at my daddy to see how my words affected him. Then I continued: "Like the other day when Mrs. Graves read to us about Frederick Douglass."

In my mind's eye, I could see my third grade teacher standing in the middle of the classroom, a calm, steady smile on her lips.

"Mrs. Graves told us that Frederick Douglass was so hungry for knowledge that he tricked some white kids into teaching him how to read. She said he was a real smart black man who used what he learned to get his freedom. He used what he learned to escape from slavery."

"Listen here, boy." Daddy seemed ruffled. "I don't give a damn about Frederick Douglass!" As he spoke, he slapped his hands against his thighs. His eyes, always serious, had an agitated look. He put his face close to mine until we were almost nose to nose. He was breathing hard, and his words came out harsh and demanding. He looked like he expected me to give him answers to his questions.

"Can Frederick Douglass help me deal with these here hard times, where money is shorter than hair on a bald man's head? Can Frederick Douglass give me some ideas about how to go out and meet the man so I can earn a dollar? No, he can't do a damn thing. Frederick Douglass is dead—stone dead, do you hear? And so are them crazy ideas he teaches from that damn book."

"But Daddy," I countered, "the teacher said that when we grow up, we should be like Frederick Douglass."

Although they were reckless, the words rushed out of my mouth so fast, I couldn't control them.

"She said we should be hungry for knowledge, that we should study real hard so we can learn more than just how to pick cotton and pull some weeds. She said the world won't have no place for people who don't know how to read, how to write, and how to count."

"You know what I think, boy?" Daddy twisted his lips into a sardonic grin. "I think you're just plumb lazy. I think you're just shucking me. I think you're using that old red book you got there to keep from doing some work."

"But Daddy, I want to read. I like to read."

When I spoke up like this to my daddy, he must have thought I was sassing him. I saw that he was beginning to grit his teeth, and I could see those ugly veins rising in his temples once again.

"I'm going to tell you one thing, boy. I want you to put that book down right this minute and get on up from there."

"But Daddy, I want to finish this book!"

Although I was filled with fear, I tried to put a determined look on my face. "Did you hear what I said, boy? I ain't going to tell you no more!" Daddy took a step towards me with a menacing glare in his eyes.

"The next time I say something to you, boy," he said, "my belt is going to do all the talking."

Chapter Six

I left the house later that Saturday morning and walked around in a daze. Daddy's bad talk about knowledge and his threat to whip me if I didn't put my book down had upset me and made me glad to be leaving the house.

I think I got out just in time, too, because I could see Daddy fingering the loops of his trousers. I knew from past experience just how quickly he could slip that belt out and use it like a whip.

I must have walked a block or two before I met up with Billy Crawford and T. J. Cook. It had been some weeks since I had accused these two fellows and Charlie Brown of stealing Daddy's money. Because the passing of time had cooled my suspicions, and because I wanted to forget my most recent encounter with my daddy, I was once again willing to talk and play with these two fellows.

"Do you want to go down to the jungle with us?" T. J. asked.

"What's down there?"

"Well, this morning real early—about eight o'clock, I guess—I happened to be looking and I saw a bunch of hobos fooling around down there. I thought it'd be a good idea to go and talk to them for a while."

"Why you want to do that?"

"Well," T. J. said, shuffling his feet, "because hobos get a chance to go all over the world. They're always on the road, and they see some things we never see in Amarillo."

"What if they try to hurt us while we're down there?" I asked.

Billy Crawford, usually a slow talker who sometimes slurred his words, answered so quickly I was surprised.

"Aw, they won't do nothing to us. Me and T. J. have been down there once before, and they didn't act like they wanted to do nothing. I thought they treated us like kings." Even though his words dropped from him like slow molasses, Billy spoke with contagious enthusiasm, and the more he talked, the more T. J. and I hooked onto the idea of making the trip to the jungle.

"The folks around here call them fellows hobos or bums," T. J. said. "But they seem to be pretty good people. No better and no worse than the grownups we see all the time. They're just trying to make it like all the other poor folks around here. I think we could learn a lot from talking to them. All we need to do is go down and sit and talk for a spell."

When we went down to the jungle, we could see five hobos standing around a fire. The five shabbily dressed men looked very much alike, even though four were white and one was black. Wearing dingy, neglected beards and hats with holes in them, the men carried bulky pouches strapped to their backs. Each man held in his hands a five-foot stick, about one inch in diameter, making them look like shepherds without sheep. The hobos had cut down some limbs and underbrush for firewood. As my playmates and I approached, we saw smoke, heard flames crackling, and smelled a delicious stew the men were cooking in an open five gallon lard can.

"How you boys doing?" one of the hobos asked as we approached.

"We're doing fine," T. J. answered. "We're all doing fine," I repeated.

"You think you boys might like having some good old beef stew?"

The black man stirring the pot chuckled as he talked. With a big grin that showed even, white teeth, he looked up briefly, but kept on stirring. As he spoke, his open face revealed a flat nose with flaring nostrils and eyes that seemed happy and contented.

"It probably ain't as good as what you'd find at home, I don't reckon, but I guess it'll be good enough to chase hunger away. Anyway, you boys are mighty welcome."

After we agreed to eat with the hobos, three of them reached into their pouches and pulled out three tin cups and three metal spoons. We eagerly took the cups and spoons, holding on to them as if they were badges of honor. For that day, at least, we felt we were hobos, too. With big grins on our faces, we could imagine ourselves traveling to Africa, Asia, and all the places around the world.

"Sorry we ain't got no napkins, boys," the black hobo said. "I guess you'll have to use the back of your hands to wipe your lips."

"That's all right," T. J. said. "We can manage."

As my friends and I sat down with the hobos on some chopped-down logs, any fear we had about them disappeared. Their honest desire to be hospitable completely disarmed us. While we were eating and relishing our stew, we felt like we were three lucky guys on a great adventure. Each of us wanted to talk with these wayward drifters to find out as much as we could about their lives.

"How long you been living as a hobo?" I asked.

The black hobo, who seemed to be the spokesman for the group, talked in a quiet voice with a strange accent. Although he was black, he didn't sound like the grownups we listened to in our neighborhood.

"I don't know about the other fellows," he said. "But I been out on the road for nearly three years. I first jumped the Acheson, Topeka, and the Santa Fe in my hometown in Kansas. You see, I couldn't find a job, so I had to hop on the road to keep myself together."

"I come from Brooklyn," one of the other hobos said. "And I guess I been hopping these freight trains going on five years now. I don't have no family, so there's nothing holding me down in one place. One day my feet got itchy, and I had to keep on the move. If I'd stayed at home, I might've gone crazy."

As we boys sat fascinated on the log-stools, each of the hobos told us something about his hometown and why he was tramping all around the country. When the last one had finished, the black hobo asked, "Now, you little fellows, what about you?" His twinkling eyes seemed to show he was enjoying our company. "What kind of story do you have?"

Each of us told the hobos how much we enjoyed the tasty stew and that we'd love to join them, to go to all the fun places they'd told us about. But I was the loudest and most persistent of all.

"If you take me with you," I said, "I'd do the dishes and all the cooking and washing. You guys wouldn't have to do nothing."

"How old are you, boy?" the black hobo asked. "Why do you want to leave home?"

"I'm eight years old," I said. "And I want to leave to get away from my daddy. He's mean to me and my mama, and I don't like him no more. All he ever thinks about is beating up on me, and he fusses all the time."

One of the hobos who hadn't talked very much spoke up in a voice that sounded like he was making an announcement. "That's a daddy's job to fuss, boy. You know what it says in the Bible, don't you?"

"Spare the rod and spoil the child!" all of us boys said in unison. Our joined voices were edged in childish sarcasm. We'd heard that biblical maxim from our parents many times before.

"Let me tell you something else, boy," the hobo from Brooklyn said. "You're wrong to be thinking about leaving your mama and daddy. I think you should go on back home where you got a warm bed and some good hot food waiting for you."

My friends and I could tell by the tone of this hobo's voice that he didn't think too much of my plan.

"Anyhow," the Brooklyn hobo continued, "riding these freight trains ain't what it's cracked up to be. It's downright dangerous. One mistake when you're trying to hop one of these babies, and wham! The wheels of the son-of-a-gun roll right over you, slicing you up like a tomato."

"Boy, I know how you feel." The black hobo smiled and put his hand on my shoulder. "A long time ago, I had a daddy just like yours. Try as hard as I could, I never did understand him—and I didn't like him either. But, you know something, boy?"

The hobo paused for a moment, putting his hand on his knee. "My old man died ten years ago, and today I miss him. I miss his bad temper, and his fussing, and his meanness. I found out the hard way that a piece of daddy is better than no daddy at all."

After this very serious comment from the black hobo, the hobo from Brooklyn broke the unexpected silence that occurred by saying, "the sun's going down, and it looks like another day is getting ready to bite the dust."

To us three boys, his words sounded very much like a hint, like he was telling us in the friendly language of hobos that it was time for us to go. So we stood up and put our utensils on the log stools. Then we went around the group, shaking each hobo's extended hand. Along with their friendly handshakes, each of the smiling men stooped down and gave us a big hug.

As we were walking away from the jungle, back towards our homes, the hobos waved and hollered at us.

"Goodbye, boys!" they said. "You all be good now. And be sure to mind your mama and daddy!"

Waving back, we yelled to them. "Thank you. Thank you for a good time! We really enjoyed ourselves!"

When we were on the street that led to the houses in our neighborhood, we were having some difficulty containing our excitement and happiness. Then T. J. said something that echoed how each of us was feeling: "I wonder why the folks in town call them fellows misfits. I think they're great guys!"

"I'd like to see them again sometimes," I said.

Chapter Seven

"**W**here have you been, boy?"

Mama's voice sounded angry, so I knew I was in trouble unless I had a good excuse for coming home just before dusk.

"You been gone all day, and I was beginning to worry about you." Her eyes glared, and the mean looking finger she pointed at me almost touched my nose.

"If you don't have a good excuse, young man, I'm going to tan your hide."

"I ain't done nothing wrong, Mama," I said. "Me, T. J. Cook, and Billy Crawford left this morning and walked down past the ice house to the jungle, near where we go frog hunting sometimes. We talked to some hobos down there. We been with them all day, listening to the good stories they had to tell."

"What do you mean you were with some hobos? Don't you know them fellows are dangerous? They could've molested or killed you boys down there. And nobody up here would know the difference."

"Mama," I said, "they didn't hurt us. They were nice to us." I looked directly into her eyes. "They gave us some food—and they talked all day about the traveling they did. Why, I'll bet they been all over the world. And you know something, Mama? One of them hobos was black. He was the smartest one in the whole bunch. He looked like he had a whole lot of book learning—and when he talked he sounded a little funny, like he didn't come from around here."

"Still, I don't want you to go down there no more, do you hear?" Mama shook her head in a disapproving way, like she wanted me to remember the seriousness of her words.

"Them hobos were good to you this time, but you don't know about the next. Every once in a while, men like them get a little out of hand. They don't have no homes and no families, and they sometimes use that as an excuse to get drunk and mean and ornery. They get mad at the world and tear up things. I don't care what you say about how good they been to you." She paused a moment to let her words sink in. "These men ain't nothing but trouble waiting, and I'll never believe they can ever be trusted."

I tried to dispel her suspicions when I said, "One of the hobos even talked me out of trying to run away, Mama." She looked at me in disbelief but I kept on talking. "When I asked if I could hop the next freight train with him and his four buddies, he told me how crazy my idea was. He told me to forget about running away, to come on back home to my mama and daddy."

"Run away?" Mama's eyes flashed, like she couldn't believe what she was hearing.

"I didn't know you were thinking about running away. Why you want to do something like that?"

"I wanted to run away 'cause I hate my daddy," I said. The words came tumbling out and I was shocked at how brutal and mean and full of anger they sounded. But I wanted to make sure Mama knew how I felt. "I'm tired of Daddy beating up on me with that old belt, and I hate him for it!"

Mama slapped me hard across my face. Although the blow stunned me, it didn't shut me up or change my mind about what I was saying.

"I hate him, Mama! I do! He beats up on me all the time. Every time I turn around, I have to be dodging that belt."

Mama lifted her hand to slap me again. But maybe she realized that I was prepared to take the blow without flinching. So she grabbed me and pulled me to her. While my head lay on her bosom, Mama wept and caressed the back of my head.

"Oh, son," she said. "Don't you see how bad that is? Can't you hear how awful that sounds? To hate your own daddy? I can't think of nothing worse."

All at once, I asked: "Mama, why is Daddy so mean? Why is he so hard to get along with?"

Mama sat down on the couch and rubbed her hands together. She couldn't hide the sad look on her face.

"Son," she said finally, "your daddy's not mean. He's just misunderstood. He's a man who stays to himself a lot, and there's something about him that makes it hard for people to get to know him. But he's not mean." Mama kept talking to me slowly, to make sure I heard every word she said.

"He's really just as kind as he can be—a gentle man who'd do anything in the world for you. But he's been hurt himself so many times in his life until sometimes he feels like trying to get even. Like today when he came home. Something happened on his job between him and one of the white men he works with. He couldn't let his temper go and tell the white man what he really thought; so when he came home, the memory of what had happened must've been straddling his back. I guess he took it out on you."

"Mama," I said. "I don't think that's fair. Daddy shouldn't have been bothering me. He should've told that white man what he wanted to say."

"Oh, no, son. It's too dangerous for a black man to do something like that. If your daddy had hit that old white piece of trash with that shovel, like he wanted to do, them white folks would've been out here with some guns and a rope."

Mama took both my hands in hers. "Zeke's a good man, son—but he's awfully hot-headed sometimes, and when he got mad today, he really wanted to lay that white man out. He really wanted to put his fists upside the man's old, ugly white head. But—he just gritted his teeth and closed his mouth, and barely managed to walk away."

Mama dropped my hands and stood up.

"But your daddy was hurt, I tell you. He was hurt, and his manhood was yanked away, like you would yank a bone away from a hungry dog. Your daddy believes a man is not supposed to cry—but I know after that thing happened on the job today, with all that lip from that white man, your daddy was crying inside. When he came home, son, you happened to be in the wrong place at the wrong time."

"Daddy never talks to me about things like that, Mama." I stood up and she pulled me closer, and caressed me again.

"All he can think about," I said, "is hitting me with that belt. And he's not like you, Mama. Whenever he sees me with a book, he makes fun." Shaking my head from side to side, I felt like laughing and crying at the same time. "Daddy makes me feel like crawling under the rug, Mama. And what's so bad about everything, he doesn't want to see me learn. He just wants me to grow up dumb and doing the same kind of work he's doing."

When she spoke again, Mama's eyes glistened, and her whole demeanor seemed to overflow with sorrow.

"Your daddy's a little shortsighted, son. I can't ever stop loving him, but perhaps better than anybody, I can see his faults. He don't have no vision. He's blind in the mind and he can't see. He can't make himself believe that, sooner or later, we black folks are going to see some better times in our lives. God don't like ugly, so things ain't going to be like this forever. Your daddy ain't learned how to trust education and knowledge. He believes that when a black man shows he's got some brains, he's just being a fool, setting himself up one more time for some evil-hearted white man to knock him down. That's why he gets upset when he sees you with your nose in a book. The kind of life he's led makes him skittish about books and book learning. When he tells you to stop all that reading, he thinks he's right. He thinks he's protecting you."

"Where's Daddy now, Mama?"

"He had to go over to Lubbock for some work he heard about. Doctor Brown needed some yardwork done on his big place up there, and since the job's going to take a while, your daddy told me he won't be back until tomorrow."

"Mama, I can't help the way I feel about Daddy," I said. "I just can't help it."

"Son," Mama said, "don't say you hate your daddy. You don't hate him. You just don't understand him. Your daddy's got lots of faults, but he's got a good heart, and he's a good provider. I know you might not believe it now, but in spite of what he says and does, your daddy loves you."

"Mama, what can I do to make Daddy show he likes me a little?"

Mama looked like she might begin to cry, and seeing her with welled-up tears in her eyes made me feel sad.

"You and me, we got to be patient with your daddy, son," she said. "It don't matter if he talks against books and black folks with learning. Don't you listen. You just keep right on working with your studies at school. You just keep right on reading all them good books. You just keep on filling that little head of yours with knowledge, okay?"

"Yes ma'am," I said.

"If you keep on studying, one of these days, your daddy is going to come to his senses. He's going to see the light one of these days, do you hear? He's going to wake up one of these days and be proud of you just as I am. Just you wait!"

Mama put her hands on my shoulders and said, "Okay, little man. I'm going to let you go now. You keep yourself busy while I go in the kitchen and whip you up some supper."

When she went to the kitchen, I stepped over to the couch, flipped on the lamplight, and picked up my old dog-eared book. I scooted down on the floor under the lamp, rolled over on my belly and began to read.

Chapter Eight

Although my face still stung from Mama's hard slap, I slept good that night. I dreamed I was a hobo—like the black hobo I had seen the previous day. In my dream, I could see myself dressed in shabby clothes, wearing a beard, and carrying a pouch on my back. I could see myself hopping freight trains and traveling from place to place, learning all kinds of things, just having myself a ball.

After I woke up, I sat on my cot and finished that old book Mama had given me. Then I put it away under my cot. No longer having that book to read, I felt a little lonely, like I was saying goodbye to an old friend. I didn't think this cloud of regret would leave until I found myself another book right away. I needed a book so I could find myself another hero and another villain.

While I dressed, I could hear Mama moving around in the kitchen. When I went to where she was, I saw that she was boiling some grits and frying some eggs and salt pork. As I sat at the table, I asked Mama when she was going to be needed out at Miss Millie's house again.

"I'm going down to her place in a couple of weeks," Mama said.

"Do you think she might have some more good books like The Count of Monte Cristo?" I asked.

"I don't rightly know, son. But when I go, I'll ask. She's always reading some book or other. When she finishes them, she just tosses them away." Mama placed three eggs cooked sunny-side-up on a platter. Then she opened the cupboard and took out a bowl, which she used to hold the steaming, white grits. She put the grits, the eggs and the cooked salt pork on the table.

"Lord," she continued, "I don't understand these rich old white ladies. They have so much money stashed away everywhere. They don't ever have to worry about trying to save."

"What time is Daddy coming home?"

"He's supposed to come later this afternoon, unless he ran into some problems on his job. When he comes, son, I want you to do something for me." Mama turned away from the stove and sat down at the table right next to me. Her face was so close, I could smell her perfume. "I want you to sit down and try to talk to your daddy, do you hear?"

I frowned at her. "Mama, do I have to do that? The only thing Daddy really likes is twanging on that old guitar of his. If he's not doing that, then he's listening to the fights or to some old Amos 'n 'Andy show on the radio. When I sit with him, he makes me feel like I ain't welcome. He shoos me away by finding some errand to send me on."

When I noticed the sudden look of displeasure on Mama's face, I got rid of my crankiness and tried to erase the petulance from my voice and the rude impudence from my demeanor. I sounded almost pleasant when I said, "I tell you what, Mama. When Daddy comes home today, I'm going to see if he will let me stay around him. Maybe I'll even ask him to go frog hunting with me sometimes."

"He might go with you if you ask him," she said. She reached across the table and took my hands in hers. "But I do want you to talk to your daddy when he comes."

She patted my hands two or three times.

"I want you to see him like I do. I want you to be around him more so you can find out for yourself that although he may use that belt too much, your daddy is really a good man."

I tried to smile so Mama would have a good reason to believe I'd do my part to become my daddy's friend.

"Anyway," Mama continued. "This evening, instead of having church services here, the pastor and the brothers and sisters are going to the Regional Convocation that's being held over in Clarendon. I'm going with them. We're going to drive up there in ten cars, so we should help them pack the place."

She smiled at me again and patted me on my head. Then she got up from the table and went over to the stove to make sure that she had turned it off.

After mama fed me my breakfast, she spent the rest of the day getting her things ready for the Convocation. She told me this big get-together of all the Saints was going to last four days. That's why she packed such a big suitcase and put enough clothes in it to last for more than a week.

About four o'clock that evening, she came to the front room, dressed in a nicely pleated dark-blue skirt, a white blouse, and a light-blue hat. She asked me how she looked. I let her know that I thought she looked all right, and she said she wanted me to walk with her over to the church, where the cars making the trip were lining up. As we walked, I carried Mama's suitcase. When I noticed it was kind of heavy, I asked, "What in the world do you have in here, Mama, the whole house?"

"No," Mama answered with a chuckle. "I just threw some things together to make myself look presentable when we get to Clarendon."

The church was about a block from where we lived, so as we made our way, Mama, stepping gingerly in her flat-heel shoes, continued to talk about Daddy.

"Your daddy should be coming home before it gets dark tonight. He knows about the trip that me and the Saints are taking. But I want you to remember to tell him I cooked a real good supper for him and that it's ready inside the oven. Do you think you can do that?"

"Yes, ma'am," I said. "That'll be easy. I ain't too hungry right now, but I will be when Daddy comes. Maybe while we're at the table eating, I can talk to him a little."

"You do that, son," Mama said. Then, when she noticed that the brothers and sisters were boarding the lined-up cars, she stooped down and motioned for me to come closer.

"Okay, my little man, I want you to come on over here and give me a kiss and a great big hug."

I fell into Mama's arms. Before she got into a big blue 1940 Dodge, she tugged gently at both my ears and hugged and kissed me three or four times. When the cars started moving from in front of the church, I trotted beside the caravan, waving and keeping up with the Dodge. Smiling broadly enough to show all her teeth, Mama sat in the back seat next to the open window. As the cars kept moving, Mama kept on waving and smiling, and so did I.

Chapter Nine

After I trotted beside Mama in the caravan of cars leaving the church, I stood on the church grounds for a while, just walking aimlessly, going from one end of the church to the other. Then I decided to walk back down to my house. When I got there, I found a group of my buddies playing touch football. They needed another body to make up a team, so I agreed to play a while. Usually, our teams were made up on the spur of the moment, just four fellows a piece, and we played on the unpaved street. Running plays back and forth on the street was really a lot of fun. When we threw passes or made touch tackles, we made the dust fly so high that when we went inside, we had to shake our clothes.

I had been playing about twenty minutes or more when I looked up. About a half block away, I saw Daddy. As he usually did, he walked fast, his arms swinging back and forth, and his legs pumping vigorously as he took his long strides. He had his black, metal lunch bucket in his left hand and a cardboard box tied with a thick white string in his right. He wore a brown woolen cap and a loose-fitting blue cotton jacket. When I spotted him, I left the game. As soon as I got close enough for him to hear, I called out, "Hi, Daddy!"

"How are you, son?" he answered. As usual, he had a serious look on his face. He didn't smile as he gazed at me.

"Mama went to the big church meeting in Clarendon, and she told me to tell you that supper's in the oven." I was trying to walk with my daddy, but because his strides were so long, I had some trouble keeping up.

"Did you know about the meeting, Daddy?"

"Yes, son. I knew about it. Your mama ain't been able to talk about nothing else for more than a week. Sometimes I think that woman's married more to that church than she is to me." Daddy smiled, which is something he didn't often do. I just assumed he had just made a private joke, so I tried to put a happy look on my face. "Anyway, you better stop playing ball and come on in now," he said. "It's getting a little dark out here."

When Daddy saw I was having some trouble keeping up with him, he slowed down a bit. Then he turned and asked, "Did you have your dinner yet?" I was practically running now as I tried to keep up. "No Sir. I was waiting for you."

As we were eating the still-warm black-eyed peas, cornbread, fried chicken and mustard greens that Mama had prepared, I blurted out, "Daddy, why don't you like me?"

My daddy's jaw dropped. He gritted his teeth, and as he began to talk, he looked like he was trying to hide the startled look on his face.

"What makes you think I don't like you, son?" When he said this, I could see a sad look on his face. I could hear a tinge of sorrow in his voice.

"Because you never talk to me," I said. "You never let me do things with you. Whenever I want to get close to you, you chase me away."

"Son, you know me. I'm a quiet man. I can't help it. That's just the way I am. I ain't never learned to let my feelings show." Daddy reached under the seat of the chair and pulled it closer to the table. "I learned a long time ago that it don't pay to let anybody get too close. I protects myself. I keep everybody at arm's length. That way, when something bad happens, I ain't never surprised because something bad is just what I expected."

I remembered what Mama told me about really trying to talk to Daddy, so becoming bolder than I'd ever been with him in the past, I asked: "But Daddy, why you have to whip me so much? Every time I make a mistake, big or small, I see you reaching for your belt."

"Well, son, I was brought up in the time when a good whipping is what a young boy learned to expect. I was taught that a good whipping made you grow."

"But Daddy, it ain't right to whip me when I do something small, or something that don't amount to much."

"Wait, wait a minute now. Let me finish, okay?" My daddy nodded, like he was getting ready to concede a point. "I reckon when I thinks about it, maybe I have been whipping you too much. But, son, I don't ever want you to think that I don't love you—because I do. I know you don't believe it, but every time I laid some licks on you, it hurt me more than it hurt you. I was only doing what my daddy did for me. When I was whipping you, I was trying to help you become a better boy and, later on, a better man."

"But Daddy, couldn't you just talk to me once in a while? Do you always have to pull out that old belt and start whipping me with it?"

"Well, son, I can only go by the lights I know. My daddy never hesitated to put his big belt on my back, and I do believe—to this day—that every lick the old man laid on me was an act of love."

When I saw that, in one little talk, I wasn't going to succeed in making Daddy change his mind about whipping me, I decided to venture into territory that was even more dangerous. I was more than a little scared as I said, "Daddy, Mama told me about how mad you got at that white man on the job the other day."

"Yeah, that old bastard told me that he couldn't stand a serious nigger." Daddy put a smirk on his face and stony sarcasm in his voice. His whole demeanor seemed to mock the white man. "I tell you, son, I got so mad, sweat was coming out of my nose and ears. You know, it wasn't what he said so much that bothered me. It was I couldn't tell him what I wanted to. I couldn't do to him what I wanted to do. I wanted to kick his butt so hard he'd have trouble sitting down for a week. I wanted to conk him over the head with that shovel I was carrying."

When Daddy said the word "conk," he thrusts his fists upward, like he was throwing an uppercut at his unseen and absent opponent. "But, because I love you and your mama, I kept my mouth shut. I just walked away."

"Why did you have to walk away, Daddy?"

"I had to walk away because I want to live—for myself and my family. I don't want to be strung up to some god-forsaken tree with a fire burning under me. And another thing, son, when you ask me why I had to walk away, you show you don't know what a black man needs to know to make it nowadays."

"What do I need to know, Daddy?"

"You need to know that I'm out there on some job busting my butt every day, at risk to my life and limb, bumping heads with them crackers at every turn."

I had never heard Daddy use such bitter words before when he talked about white folks, so I sat there listening to him, spellbound, too startled at that moment to say anything. His face looked angrier and angrier, as he continued.

"The white folks I know, they're really some mischievous people. I wouldn't trust any of them as far as I can throw this house. It makes no difference how nice they can pretend to be sometimes. It don't matter how big a smile they got on their faces. You really got to watch them, because if you turn your back on them, every time they end up tricking you. That's why I get so upset with you, son."

A look of scorn flickered across my daddy's face.

"You don't know nothing about white folks. Absolutely nothing! And you don't do a damn thing to try to learn!"

With his elbow on the table, Daddy moved his right, balled-up fist up and down. He looked like he had a sledge hammer, and he sounded like every word he said was a stake that he was trying to drive into the ground.

"No, you think you can learn everything you need to know by sticking your nose in some damn book. You don't realize that books ain't really no good for you. You don't know that reading what's in them books too much will make you feel like you got some promise. But later on, when you get bold enough to want to show that promise, some old hoary-headed cracker will come along, and he'll take that promise, whatever it is, and shove it down your throat."

"But Mama and all my teachers keep telling me that knowledge is sweet. They said that if I get a good education, I can build myself a good future, and one day I can get a good job. When I talk to her, Mama tells me that, one of these days, things are going to get better for us black folks here in Amarillo. She says that all we have to do is be patient and keep on learning and improving ourselves. One day, Mama says, we'll be able to do anything them white folks can do."

"You know something, son?" My daddy chuckled and cleared his throat. "I think you and your mama are just plumb crazy—crazy as a couple of bed bugs." My daddy pushed his chair back and stood up from the table. He had a look of quiet resignation on his face, and as he stood, he rocked back and forth, like he wasn't quite sure what he was going to do next.

"I guess I'm an old dog and you can't teach me new tricks. I am what I am because of what I've seen. I can't rightly expect you to be like me. Boy, maybe your mama ain't so crazy after all. Maybe she's right. Maybe life does hold more promise for you than it gave to me." After my daddy stood up, he started walking toward the front of the house. He used his right hand to invite me to come with him. "Come on into the front room, little fellow," he said. "I got something for you."

When we got to the front room, Daddy pointed at the box that he had been carrying. "Dr. Brown put some things in this box that I thought you might like. You feel like you want to take a look?"

I was so excited Daddy didn't have to ask me twice. In two quick steps, I was down on my knees next to the box, scrambling to open it. When I got the box opened, I saw ten neatly stacked used books, the covers of which looked pretty good, despite being obvious hand-me-downs the doctor had given Daddy. I flipped through the pages of the first books, and when I saw the titles Kidnapped, Alice's Adventure's in Wonderland, and Through the Looking Glass, I wondered what these books were going to be about, and what they would teach me.

When Daddy saw how delighted I was to be getting these unexpected gifts, he smiled and sat down on the couch. He kept watching me examine each of the books, grinning more than I had ever seen him do. Then, when he heard a knock at the front door, he got up to see who it was. As he walked toward the door, I could barely contain my excitement. Continuing carefully to examine each book, I could tell I was really going to have some fun.

Chapter Ten

When my daddy opened the front door, I heard the low but clear voice of Elder Lemuel Jones, the pastor of the church. He seemed to be trying to whisper to my daddy, so I could barely hear him.

"Brother Zeke," the pastor said. "I'd like to talk to you for a minute—alone. Can you come out here for a spell? Please, brother, if you don't mind, close the door behind you."

As soon as I heard the pastor's muffled voice, I sensed that something unusual was about to happen. I put the books back into the box, wondering what in the world the pastor was doing in front of our house. He should have been in Clarendon with all the other Saints. When I saw Daddy follow the pastor's suggestion and close the front door, my natural nosiness took over. As soon as Daddy shut the door, I rushed to the window and pressed my forehead to the pane so I could see, if not hear, what was happening.

The pastor had both hands on my daddy's shoulders, and both men seemed highly agitated. I could see the pastor's lips moving, but because his head was so close to my daddy's ears, I couldn't make out what he was saying. But I did see and hear Daddy when, suddenly, he started jumping up and down and shouting, "Oh, no! no, no, God, no, no!"

Then, although he was not usually a religious man, Daddy raised both his arms skyward, like he wanted to make a supplication to heaven. "Oh, God," he said in the most plaintive voice I had ever heard him use. "Why did you have to let it happen?"

When I heard and saw all the commotion, I opened the door and rushed outside. I saw Daddy and the pastor, both of them big husky men, rocking back and forth, embracing each other. The pastor, who apparently had no compunctions about men shedding tears, was crying shamelessly. Although he was clearly distressed, Daddy looked like he was comforting the pastor. He told him, "Thank you, Pastor Jones, for letting me know. Thank you. I better go tell the boy myself."

When my daddy saw I had disregarded his silent command and had opened the front door to come outside, he looked at me with the saddest look I'd ever seen on his face. I was surprised but happy when I didn't see any anger. In the past, whenever I disobeyed him, a cold, uncompromising fury would be the first thing I would see in his face. This time he just gazed at me with a faraway look, and he kept rubbing his tongue across his teeth and over his lower lip. As Daddy moved his lips to speak to me, he seemed to be having trouble getting the words out. Then, finally, very gently for him, he held both my hands. In a sad voice, he said, "Come on back into the house, son. I got something to tell you."

Inside, we both sat down on the couch. Daddy, still holding my hands, told me the bad news. "Son, the car your mama was riding in had an accident tonight. The pastor said the driver was trying to keep from having a head-on collision, and he swerved off the road. Unfortunately, when the car swerved, the back door flew open, and your mama was killed when she was thrown from the back seat." Releasing the tight grip he had on my hands, my daddy blinked his eyes and then reached into his pocket and pulled out a white handkerchief. Then he folded it in half before he took it and blew his nose. After putting the handkerchief back into his pocket, Daddy grabbed my hands again. He looked into my eyes and spoke softly.

"Your mama died right there on the highway, so they didn't waste any time taking her to the hospital. They took her straight to the mortuary."

I couldn't believe what Daddy told me. My mama dead? No, no, that couldn't be, I thought. Not that. I looked at my daddy and he seemed confused and unsettled. His swollen eyes had become misty, but he was not crying. I looked directly into his face, and when I saw him gritting his teeth, I realized, suddenly, that Mama really was dead, and I started bawling. I couldn't help myself, and for a moment, I thought I was going to choke from grunts and tears.

"Okay, son, you go ahead now and get that crying out of your system. Do it now while nobody's around." As he said this, Daddy let his voice rise so that it revealed an urgency he didn't try to hide. Then he put both his big hands on my shoulders, and very slowly and gently, he drew my weeping head to his chest. He patted the back of my neck and the back of my head, and made circular movements on my back with the palms of his hands.

"Son, I want you to cry until you dry up all them tears, until there ain't one of them left. I want you to cry now, because later, I want you to be a little man."

He couldn't seem to keep his voice from rising. Then for some reason, he doubled up both his fists and looked for a moment as if he was going to pound them angrily on his knees.

"I want you to show all these here folks in Amarillo that you're a strong little boy and that you know how to bear your pain—every bit of it—without whining or moping around."

"But Daddy, how can I do that?" I bawled as I pulled away from him. "I just lost my mama. Why can't I cry?"

"I know how you feel, son. I wish it could be all right for you to go boo-hooing around. But, in this here world, things ain't never what they ought to be." Daddy looked at me sternly, and he began to grit his teeth again.

"When these here folks see you crying, they going to look and see only your weakness. The next thing they'll try to do is walk all over you."

"But Daddy, how am I going to keep from crying?" I insisted.

"I don't know what to tell you, son. All I do know is us men don't have the luxury of shedding tears. If you was a girl, you could cry. If you was a woman, you could cry. But as a boy, a man-child, one thing you got to learn very fast is how to hide your feelings." He shook his head and used his upper teeth to scrape across his bottom lip.

"You got to look upon how you feel inside as the most secret part of yourself, which you don't ever want to expose to nobody." Daddy raised both hands and rubbed them, palms down, over the top of his head. Then with his thumb and forefinger, he rubbed his eyes gently, blinking quickly before he spoke. "If you want to become a strong man when you grow up, you got to learn now that it's best to keep your pain to yourself."

"Daddy, I don't know if I can do it."

"You got to do it, son. For me and your mama."

Then Daddy stood up. He was still rubbing his tongue over his upper and lower lips, like they were dry and he was trying to keep them moist. He rubbed his hands on his thighs and ran his fingers through the loops of his pants. Reaching down on the couch to pick it up, he put his cotton jacket back on. "I got to go down to the mortuary now. I want to see your mama."

"Can I go with you, Daddy?"

"No, son. I'm sorry, but you can't go. They don't allow nobody but grownups down there. This is something I got to do alone."

As I watched my daddy walk through the front door, I began to whimper and moan. Daddy gazed back at me for a moment with a look of gloomy displeasure on his face. Then, with his usual big strides, he walked away.

Chapter Eleven

That night, after I found out Mama was dead, I tried to cry myself to sleep. But sleep wouldn't come. I turned and tossed on my little cot and my eyes just wouldn't close.

Then I started thinking about Mama and something came to my mind that I thought I had forgotten. It was something that happened many years earlier, when I was just four years old.

I was pedaling my tricycle hard. My chubby legs pumped furiously, and as I bent my body toward the handlebars of my trike, I kept my eyes glued to the asphalt road in front of me. Although the speeding cars coming from the opposite direction made droning, bee-like sounds as they whizzed by, the eerie roaring didn't upset me. I just kept up my rhythmic pedaling, stopping only every now and then.

One time when I stopped, I twisted my body to look behind me. When I didn't see Mama, I got scared, but I didn't stop and I didn't cry. I returned to my frantic pedaling. Although I couldn't see Mama, I felt it would be better for me to keep on pumping.

I guess I thought that maybe something would happen and she would show up later. Sweat began to drop from my body, moistening my forehead and dampening the back of my shirt. As I pedaled, I made a whirring noise with my clinched teeth and tongue, creating a sound that seemingly came from deep within my throat. To get rid of my panic, I pretended that I was driving a great big car like the one I once saw my daddy drive.

After a while, when I thought I must have been pedaling forever, a car lurched up behind me, honking, with the motor still running. Startled at first, I stopped and twisted the front wheel of my trike toward the curb. Then I turned around so that I could see what was happening. That's when I spotted Mama getting out of the shiny, black car that had zoomed up behind me. Seeing her made me relax, and when I noticed she was smiling, I stopped making the whirring sound and dropped my hands to my side.

"I didn't think you'd ever realize I wasn't walking behind you, son," Mama said, with a touch of pride in her voice. "Didn't you get scared? Didn't you miss your mama at all?"

"Yes ma'am, I missed you," I said. "And I did get scared a little, but I just kept on pedaling."

Mama told me to get off my trike so she could pick it up and put it in the trunk of the car. "My goodness! You're a brave, little fellow." She slammed shut the trunk of the car. "Come on up here, sweetheart, and sit in front between me and Sister Jones."

I made my way to the front seat next to Sister Jones, the pastor's wife. Mama smiled at me and patted me lightly on the back of my head. Then she said, "Let's go on home now. I got to tell all the folks back there how you didn't stop. You kept on going. Even when you thought you was lost, you kept on going, and you didn't cry."

As the car barreled down the road, Mama snuggled me next to her and hugged my shrugging shoulders. Then she said, "Son, I'm really proud of you. I just know you're going to grow up and be a really strong man one day."

With my eyes wide from deeply felt joy, and smiling broadly, I looked up at my mama. Squirming in my seat, I put my hand on her left knee . . . .

Hours must have passed after this memory flickered across my mind. This was an incident that happened between me and Mama a long time ago, and I wondered why would I think of it now. I had a deep-down gut feeling that something or somebody was telling me Daddy was right after all. I had to stop my crying. I had to make Mama proud. That night, I made a promise to myself. "From now on, I don't care what happens," I said. "I'm going to be my mama's little man, and I ain't going to cry."

After I made this decision, I got very drowsy, and fell into a deep sleep.

Chapter Twelve

When we first got up that morning, four days after we found out Mama was dead, Daddy told me to go outside and be on the lookout for the hearse. With my hands in my pockets, I stood in front of my house, watching. When the big, black hearse appeared, I knew Mama would be inside. My stomach churned, and I didn't want to watch as the funeral-home attendants lugged Mama's casket inside the house. Biting the inside of my upper lip, I crouched behind a parked car until those men wearing white gloves and black uniforms, had delivered the casket and were driving off.

As I walked toward the house, I focused on how I was acting. I knew the neighbors, aware of Mama's death, would be watching just to see how I behaved. I took a deep breath and tried to walk straight and be as calm as I could.

As I climbed the steps, I saw Daddy in the doorway, holding the screen door open. Wearing an old black suit he had pressed, he seemed ill at ease. The tightly fitting red tie bouncing around on his Adam's apple, made him look like he might choke if he wasn't careful.

"Son, you'd better come on in now." Daddy placed his hands on my shoulders. 'Tuck your shirttail in and go wash up a bit. Then you can go see your mama."

"Yes, Sir," I said. When I stumbled into the front room, I rushed to the bathroom, feeling like I might upchuck at any moment.

What was happening to me? I felt like somebody was holding the muscles of my legs and wouldn't let me walk in a normal, regular way. In front of the mirror over the wash basin, I shook my legs in an attempt to wake them up. Nothing seemed to work. My legs continued to feel dull and sleepy and I couldn't seem to make that queasy feeling in my stomach go away.

After I washed up, combed my hair, and put my shirttail in, I saw the copper-covered casket in the living room on a large, rectangular mahogany table. The casket lay open, so I stepped over and peered inside. Mama seemed to be asleep. Lying on top of some gray satin sheets, she wore a white blouse and a stiff blue cotton skirt. Somebody had placed a white carnation in her freshly straightened hair. She looked like she was smiling, even though none of her teeth showed. With her eyes closed and her hands folded over her chest, Mama looked peaceful, like she'd escaped all the troubles of this world. I reached into the casket and touched Mama's right cheek. It was hard and cold, so I yanked my hand back.

During the time Mama lay in the funeral home, I missed her. I couldn't believe I would never see her again. Most of the wonderful things about Mama that I could remember seemed to be connected in some way to food, and when I closed my eyes, I could see her setting the table.

"Son," my daddy said as he approached me. "A lot of people are going to be here today for your mama's wake." As he talked, his lips moved in a slow, deliberate way. The way he had of stressing certain words—so that they stood out above the others—seemed more pronounced than in the past. He looked like he was struggling to get each word out. "All your mama's friends want to see her one more time here at home. She's in the front room now, but when that hearse comes back in a few hours, they'll be taking her to the church for the funeral."

"Yes, Sir," I said.

"We're the only ones left in the family now, son, and I want you to remember what I told you the other night." Stooping to embrace me, Daddy spoke to me in a low voice. "When it's time for us to go to the funeral, I want you to be strong. I know you just lost your mama and you're going through a lot of pain. But like I told you, son—I want all them folks to see a little man out there today. Me and your mama will be proud. That's why I don't want you to cry. You can do it, son. I know you can! You can do it if you remember that your mama's in heaven watching you."

"Yes Sir." I bit my bottom lip, struggling to stifle the urge to sob. "I can do it."

Mama would have liked her funeral. About 100 people crowded into the church, using all the available pews. The choir sang some beautiful songs, and Sister Beulah Johnson sang "Amazing Grace" with such enthusiasm and relish that, as she sang, the brothers and sisters jumped up, clapped their hands, and started shouting, "Hallelujah! Hallelujah!" The whole church rocked from the singing and the shouting, and I know Mama would have liked it when the people in the church made such a joyful noise unto the Lord. She would have been pleased.

The pastor, Elder Lemuel Jones, preached a sermon that made me realize just how much everybody loved and appreciated Mama. In his sermon, the pastor said,

"Sister Thelma was a real wonderful Christian lady, a dutiful wife and a wise and loving mother. She's gone on home now, but in many ways, brothers and sisters, she's still alive. Her spirit's still here. By way of her good deeds and unselfishness, she's left a copy of herself behind." The pastor thumped the pulpit with both fists and waved his hands above his head. "I'm so glad to tell you that while Sister Thelma lived, she saw and rejoiced. And when she died, because of the wonderful life she lived, she had no regrets."

I could tell that what the pastor said touched the whole congregation, and when I looked to my left along the long pew I was sitting in, I saw my granddaddy, my mama's father, his black face gleaming. With both his arms folded across his chest, he was shaking his head from side to side, with tears streaming down his cheeks. I just kept telling myself, "I'm a big boy and I ain't going to cry."

And I didn't either, even when everybody stood and filed past Mama's coffin. I didn't cry, even though I could feel the urge coming from underneath my toes and creeping upwards over my whole body. The urge was nearing my chest, and I was hoping that I'd be able to hold out before the powerful throbbing reached my throat.

The funeral went smoothly until Aunt Sulla, my mama's sister, passed Mama's casket. When Aunt Sulla, with sobs shaking her body, got in front of the casket, she stopped. Then, with cat-like movements, she tried to climb inside. Because she was a stocky woman, about five feet eight inches tall and 140 pounds, when Aunt Sulla tried to grab Mama's shoulders, she made the casket tilt. The pastor and the whole congregation watched in shock, as the casket rocked slowly back and forth.

Suddenly a resounding thump shook the whole building as the ushers and the funeral home attendants rushed to the tilting casket to catch it before it came crashing down. They reached it in time and two ushers peeled my weeping aunt off my mama's shoulders and dragged her, arms flailing, back to the pew where she'd been sitting. As all this commotion took place, a loud shrill, anonymous voice, rebounding from the ceiling, shrieked from somewhere in the back of the church. "Oh Lordy! Lord! This family needs you!" the voice boomed. "Bless this family, Lord!"

After the funeral, in a procession that included the hearse and about fifteen cars, we took Mama's casket to the gravesite. When we got there, four grave-diggers in coveralls stood by, ready to use two woven leather belts to lower their heavy burden into the grave. Before we left the gravesite, the pastor put his hands on the casket, prayed, and said a few more words of farewell. Then my daddy, aunt, granddaddy, and all of Mama's relatives and friends covered the casket with white roses and carnations. Then I walked up to the casket and placed on the lid the note I had struggled early that morning to write. I had folded the note so nobody but me could see where, in my very best printing, I'd written a private message that said simply, "Mama, I love you because you taught me knowledge is sweet."

Later that night, as I lay on my small cot, I thought of all that had happened that day. I remembered hiding behind the car to avoid seeing the hearse. I remembered touching Mama's cheek as the casket sat in the house. I remembered jerking my hands away, and the shame I felt afterwards. I remembered the singing, the shouting, the pastor's sermon, and my aunt's strange behavior at the church.

Suddenly, I felt tired, tired of being a big boy, tired of not crying. I couldn't stand the hurt I felt from holding back the tears. So with my knees doubled up next to my stomach, I pulled my pillow over my head and let myself go. An avalanche of emotion overwhelmed me, and I shook so much I couldn't tell whether I was retching or crying. After a while, I got up to go to the bathroom to wash my face. When I passed Mama's and Daddy's bedroom, I heard my dad inside. He was crying, too.

CPSIA information can be obtained
at www.ICGtesting.com
Printed in the USA
FSOW01n0700200717
36655FS